Cuddles
the Cattle Dog

A New Christmas Tail

Written by Julian Frazin
Illustrated by Susan Schirmer

*O*nce upon a Christmas Eve...

Once upon a Christmas Eve...
Santa packed his toys to leave,
and as he went to put them in his sleigh,

all his elves began to shout,
"Someone let the reindeer out,
every single one has run away."

Sure enough they checked each stable,
searched as far as they were able,
there was not a reindeer to be found.

They said, "It's very hard you know,
to search for reindeer in the snow.
Maybe *'you know who'* can look around."

But Santa said,
"The nose of 'you know who'
is hard to see,

since somebody forgot to change his
9-volt battery!"

Santa Claus was in a bind,
a good reindeer is hard to find,
and he lost the only ones he had.

"Dancer! Prancer! Donner too!
Blitzen! Where the heck are you?"
Santa started looking rather sad.

Till an elf came and assured 'im,
"I know someone who can herd 'em,
a little dog I've known since she's a pup.

Her name is 'Cuddles' and she's small,
that shouldn't matter, not at all,
a cattle dog knows how to round 'em up."

Then all the other elves
began to sing and dance,
"Oh, Santa Claus,
please give that little cattle dog
a chance."

And they sang: (To the tune of "Waltzing Matilda")

*"Cuddles, the cattle dog, Cuddles, the cattle dog,
Back in Australia, she herds lots of steer..."*

First, Santa said, "No way."

But then he said –

"Okay!"

Cuddles ran out in the snow,
as the wind began to blow,
which had made it very hard to see.

Though she looked from left to right,
no reindeer came into sight.

Snow affects your visibility.

Santa Claus began to frown.
The situation got him down,
and he started having many doubts.

"If I don't find those reindeer soon,
I won't get out till half past noon.
And I'll have to cancel my
delivery routes."

"Don't worry," said one of the elves.
"That cattle dog won't fail ya.
It's just the weather's not the same,
as back home in Australia."

Then the snow began to clear.
Cuddles saw a few reindeer.
But the reindeer always ran away.

Every time that she came near,
another one would disappear.
That's when an elf stood up and said, "G'day."

The elf said, "Sydney is 'me' name,
which incidentally is the same,
back home in Australia as 'me' town.

I've worked with herders, red and blue.
There's a little trick we do,
to get those Aussie dogs to settle down.

I have this little whistle, and on it I will blow.
Then that little cattle dog will know
which way to go."

"From the signal that I blow,
Cuddles knows which way to go.
Right or left,
she'll take off like a missile.

Backward, forward... watch that pup,
as she rounds those reindeer up."

Then he took a breath and blew
– "toot-tweet!" – his whistle.

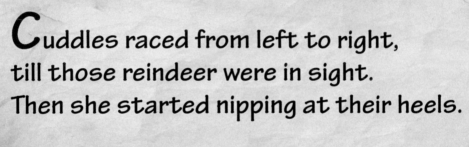

Cuddles raced from left to right,
till those reindeer were in sight.
Then she started nipping at their heels.

Soon they all came into view,
Dasher, Dancer, Prancer too,
just in time to have their evening meals.

Vixen, Blitzen, Comet, Cupid, here comes
Donner too... every one of Santa's reindeer,
rounded up by –   'you guess who.'

Now each year on Christmas Eve,
as Santa packs his toys to leave,
that little cattle dog is at his side.

Making sure the reindeer stay,
in their place and not stray.

Then Santa lets her hop in for a ride.

As Santa starts out on his way,
there's Cuddles, right there in his sleigh;
she even gets to take her fav'rite bone.

And Santa, happy as can be, says,
"Cuddles, you're good company.
Now I'll never have to make the trip alone."

So, don't be surprised if on Christmas Eve,
as you are laying in the dark,

when you close your eyes and open your ears,
you hear a little dog bark – "woof!"

If you listen closely,
you might hear a familiar song,
and if you do it very quietly,
you can even sing along.

(To the tune of "Waltzing Matilda" –
the most popular song in Australia)

"Down in Australia,
there are many cattle dogs.
You got your 'bluey' and 'red heeler' too,
and there's one so keen,
she is only seen on Chrissie Eve,
If you believe, then she'll be there for you.

Cuddles, the cattle dog,
Cuddles, the cattle dog,
Back in Australia, she herds up the steer.
And it's perfectly clear if that cattle dog
can handle steer, she'll find and round up
eight tiny reindeer."

The End!

Julian Frazin is a retired state court judge. He has written many humorous plays, popular songs and funny parodies. He and his wife Rhona split their time between homes in Chicago and Southwest Michigan with their dog Cuddles. This is his first children's book.

Julian Frazin
Author

Susan Schirmer is a Michigan native, mother of three and recently a grandmother who has a background in both fine arts and graphic arts. She is currently a studio artist at the Box Factory for the Arts in St. Joseph, Michigan, where she divides her time between creating and teaching art. Although she has had experience in illustrating for publications, "Cuddles the Cattle Dog" is her first work on a children's book.

Susan Schirmer
Illustrator

Cuddles is an Australian Cattle Dog who was rescued from the Michiana Humane Society. The most popular dog in Australia, the "Bluey" or "Red Heeler," as they are also known depending on their coloring, are intelligent, loyal, affectionate and hardworking animals bred for herding cattle. Although she served as the inspiration for this book, Cuddles has never visited Australia. And while she has never had to round up cattle, or otherwise work for a living, she has been known to bark at toll booth attendants and herd errant tennis balls and loud vacuum cleaners.

Cuddles
The Cattle Dog

Cuddles the Cattledog

(to the tune of "Waltzing Matilda")

Australia

Carefree

mf Do - wn in Aus - tra - lia, there are ma - ny cat - tle dogs,

You got your blue - y and red heeler too, and there's

one so - o keen, she's on - ly seen on Chris - sie eve,

If you be - lieve then she'll be there for you.

CHORUS

f Cud - dles the cattle dog, Cud - dles the cattle dog,

Back in Aus - tra - lia she herds up the steer, p And it's

per - fect - ly clear if that cat - tle dog can han - dle steer

f She'll find and round up eight ti - ny rein - deer.